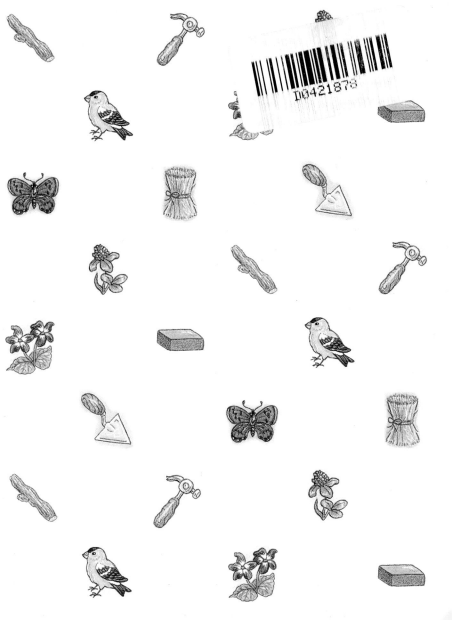

This book belongs to

_____

The
Three Little Pigs

RETOLD BY

Jennifer Greenway

ILLUSTRATED BY

Debbie Dieneman

ARIEL BOOKS

ANDREWS AND McMEEL
KANSAS CITY

Library of Congress Cataloging-in-Publication Data

Greenway, Jennifer.
    The three little pigs / retold by Jennifer Greenway ; illustrated
by Debbie Dieneman.
        p.   cm.
    Summary: The adventures of three little pigs who leave home to seek
their fortunes and how they deal with the big bad wolf.
    ISBN 0-8362-4904-6 : $6.95
    [1. Folklore. 2. Pigs—Folklore.] I. Dieneman, Debbie, ill.
II. Three little pigs. English. III. Title.
PZ8.1.G858Th   1991
398.2—dc20   91-9933
    [E]   CIP
                                                               AC

Design: Susan Hood and Mike Hortens
Art Direction: Armand Eisen, Mike Hortens, and Julie Phillips
Art Production: Lynn Wine
Production: Julie Miller and Lisa Shadid

The
Three Little Pigs

$\mathcal{O}$nce upon a time, there were three little pigs who lived in a broken-down cottage with their mother. As they were very poor, the three little pigs decided that it was none too early for them to go into the world and seek their fortunes. So the first little pig packed his favorite belongings, said good-bye to his mother, and set off.

He hadn't gone far before he came to a fine road paved with stones.

"What a beautiful road," said the first little pig. "I believe I will walk down it and see what I can find."

After a while the first little pig came upon a man carrying a big bundle of straw.

"Good morning, sir," said the first little pig. "Please sell me that bundle of straw so that I can make myself a house."

"Certainly," said the man.

So the first little pig gave the man all his money, and the man gave him the bundle of straw.

The first little pig got right to work. He lashed the straw to a coil. Then he wound the coil round and round to build up the walls. Soon the first little pig had made himself a cozy little house of straw, and he was very pleased.

But just as the first little pig was sitting down to his first supper in his new home, along came a big, bad wolf. The wolf had been hunting in the woods all day without finding anything to eat, and he was very hungry. When he saw the little pig's house, he thought, "Now I have found my supper!" The wolf knocked on the little pig's door and cried:

Little pig, little pig!
Let me in!

13

The first little pig peered out the window. When he saw the big, bad wolf, he said:

No, indeed, I won't let you in!
Not by the hair of my chinny-chin-chin!

That made the wolf cross. So he growled in a very loud voice:

Then I'll huff and I'll puff,
And I'll blow your house down!

But the first little pig still wouldn't let him in. So the big, bad wolf huffed and he puffed until the little house of straw came tumbling down. The first little pig had to run away as fast as he could, or the wolf would have surely eaten him up!

Shortly afterward, the second little pig decided it was time for him to seek his fortune. So he said good-bye to his mother and off he went.

He soon came to a road that was freshly paved with gravel. "What a nice, new road," thought the second little pig. "I believe I will walk down it and see what I can find."

So he turned onto the new gravel road.

Before long, the second little pig came upon a man carrying a big bundle of sticks.

"Good morning, sir," said the second little pig. "Please sell me that bundle of sticks so I can build myself a house."

"Certainly," said the man.

So the second little pig gave the man all his money. Then he took the bundle of sticks and got to work.

The second little pig sawed the sticks neatly. Then he nailed them together. Before long he had made himself a cozy little house of sticks.

But no sooner had the second little pig finished putting on the front door than along came the big, bad wolf.

The wolf knocked loudly at the door and cried:

Little pig, little pig!
Let me in!

When the second little pig peeked out of the window and saw the big, bad wolf, he replied:

No, indeed, I won't let you in!
Not by the hair of my chinny-chin-chin!

That made the wolf cross. So the wolf growled in a very loud voice:

Then I'll huff and I'll puff,
And I'll blow your house down!

The second little pig was frightened, but he still wouldn't let the wolf in.

So the big, bad wolf began to huff and puff.

He huffed and he puffed and he puffed and he huffed.

Before long, the big, bad wolf blew down the second little pig's house of sticks—right down to the ground.

The second little pig had to run away as fast as he could, or the big, bad wolf would have surely eaten him up!

After a while, the third little pig decided it was time for him to go into the world and seek his fortune.

So he packed his belongings and said good-bye to his mother. Then off he went.

After a while he came to a small dirt road. "What a quiet little road," the third little pig said to himself. "I believe I shall go down it and see what I can find."

So the third little pig walked down the dirt road.

Soon he came upon a man carrying a big load of bricks.

"Good morning, sir," said the third little pig. "Please sell me your load of bricks so I can build myself a house."

"Certainly," said the man.

So the third little pig gave the man all his money, and the man gave him the bricks.

The third little pig mixed up some cement, and he carefully laid the bricks one on top of the other. Before long, the little pig had built himself a cozy, sturdy little house of bricks.

No sooner had the third little pig gone inside than along came the big, bad wolf. The wolf knocked on the door as loudly as he could and cried:

Little pig, little pig!
Let me in!

But the third little pig had seen the big, bad wolf coming, and so he replied:

No, indeed, I won't let you in.
Not by the hair of my chinny-chin-chin!

The wolf was very cross when he heard that! So he growled in a big voice:

Then I'll huff and I'll puff
And I'll blow your house down!

Then the wolf huffed and puffed. And he puffed and he huffed. And he huffed and he puffed some more. But no matter how hard he tried, he could not blow down the little house of bricks! So the wolf climbed onto the roof and stuck his head down the chimney.

"I am just poking my nose inside," he said.

"As you like," said the third little pig.

"Now I am just putting my ears inside," said the wolf.

"Fine with me," said the third little pig.

"Now I am just putting my paws inside," said the wolf.

"Very well," said the third little pig.

"Now I am just putting my tail inside," said the wolf. And he fell down the third little pig's chimney!

Suddenly, the wolf gave a terrible howl, for the clever little pig had set a big kettle of water to boil in the fireplace!

The big, bad wolf had to scramble back up the chimney as fast as he could, for otherwise, he surely would have been boiled alive in the third little pig's big kettle.

And so the big, bad wolf ran away, and the third little pig lived happily ever after in his cozy, sturdy little house of bricks!